Billy the Sea Turtle

D1469382

Written and Illustrated by

Annabelle Bennett

Published by eBookIt.com
http://www.eBookIt.com

ISBN-13: 978-1-4566-3743-9

On a warm summer night in mid September,
the world was still as if to remember.

With a full moon above and stars brightly glistening,
the universe itself appeared to be listening.

With a small nudge in the sand,
two tiny fins and a nose appeared on the land.

Billy and dozens of his siblings followed the moon,
in search for the ocean they hoped to reach soon.

Billy found a home
where he began to
grow and play,
with all of his friends
along the way.

Billy and his friend, Kevin, spent their days
collecting shells and snacking on grass,
while their neighbor, Mr. Crab, would always pass.

Sometimes Kevin just swam too fast.
Not knowing why, Billy always ended up last.

One day the friends decided to swim afar,
in hopes of finding a shell-filled sandbar.

As the sun began to slowly set,
Billy and Kevin started to fret.

The water churned and the fish swam away.
Thinking Billy was behind him, Kevin sped home
leaving Billy astray.

Lost and scared in the middle of nowhere,
Billy took a deep breath of the salty fresh air.

Billy slowly woke up feeling tired and sluggish,
then found himself surrounded on all sides by rubbish.

Yet the trees were green
and the beaches so white,
not a cloud in sky ever so bright.

Far in the distance there was a girl
walking toward Billy with a bucket and a pearl.

As she drew closer, Billy leaned back to hide,
but a few more steps and she turned to her side.

She picked up a bottle and to her surprise,
she spotted itty bitty Billy with her big blue eyes.

She bent low on the ground for a closer view,
and Billy wondered who she was too.

She carefully moved Billy to the warm soft sand,
then set down her bucket to fill it with her hand.

Billy stayed still, he didn't move a thing,
and soon he realized he was now king!

The girl grabbed her shell before Billy could crawl, and all of a sudden, strings began to fall.

Billy let out a sigh
and shook off a loose end,
he had never felt better
as he looked up at his new friend.

She gave him a smile and removed all the ties,
then they gave each other loving goodbyes.

Billy then swam as fast as he could,
with a smile on his face because he now understood.

Reduce Reuse Recycle

• Reuse containers

• Use a reusable water bottle

• Only purchase what you need

• Avoid using harsh chemicals

• Check labels before you dispose of items to recycle properly

• Pick up after yourself and others, especially outside

• Volunteer for beach clean ups

• Cut up plastic bottle holder rings and masks before disposing them

• Educate others on how to better treat the environment and our oceans

• Support organizations working to protect the environment

• Act now

A Portion of the Proceeds Go To One of the Following Charities:

oceana.org

coral.org

worldwildlife.org

4ocean.com

CPSIA information can be obtained
at www.ICGtesting.com
Printed in the USA
BVHW021158290622
640915BV00002B/6